EVERY MAN
HEART
LAY DOWN

EVERY MAN HEART LAY DOWN

BY LORENZ GRAHAM
Pictures by
Colleen Browning

Boyds Mills Press

Published by Caroline House
Boyds Mills Press, Inc.
A Highlights Company
815 Church Street
Honesdale, Pennsylvania 18431
Printed in Hong Kong

Publisher Cataloging-in-Publication Data
Graham, Lorenz B.
    Every man heart lay down / by Lorenz Graham ; pictures by
Colleen Browning.
[48]p. : col. ill. ; cm.
Originally published in the author's *How God Fix Jonah*.
This book was originally published by Thomas Y. Crowell
Company, New York, in 1970.
Summary : The story of Christ's birth is retold in the striking
language of an African storyteller.
ISBN 1-56397-184-4
1. Jesus Christ—Nativity—Juvenile literature. [1. Jesus Christ—
Nativity.]
I. Browning, Colleen, ill. II. Title.
232.92—dc20   1993
Library of Congress Catalog Card Number 92-72829

The text of this book is set in 15-point Garamond.
The illustrations are done in mixed media.
Distributed by St. Martin's Press

10 9 8 7 6 5 4 3 2

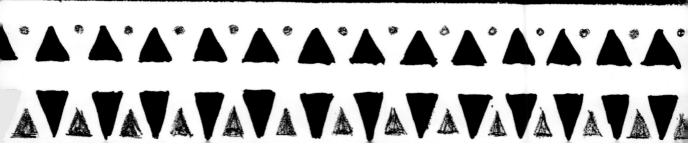

These little poems . . . are told here in the words and thought patterns of a modern African boy who does not . . . use the conventional words and phrases which by long usage often obscure the meaning of these tales in the minds of Europeans and Americans.

This is the stuff of which literature is made. . . .
—W. E. B. Du Bois

From the Foreword of *How God Fix Jonah,* a collection of stories from the Bible retold by Lorenz Graham, in which *Every Man Heart Lay Down* first appeared.

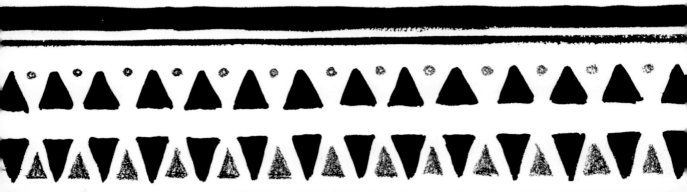

Introduction

The familiar Bible stories of kings and slaves, of strength and weakness, of love and hate were brought to Africa by missionaries. As they were retold by Africans, they took on the imagery of the people. Shepherd David with his harp of many strings, strong man Samson who was weak for woman palaver, and baby Jesus born in the place where cattle sleep are now part of the folklore of the country. To the African storyteller the Bible tale becomes a poem, or rather a spoken song. His words are simple and rhythmic. The song is sung, and it is sweet.

It was in Liberia that I first heard many of these tales, recounted in the idiom of Africans newly come to English speech. They can be heard in many other parts of the continent as well—in the west and even in the east wherever the English settlers spread their language.

Words of Spanish and Portuguese still remain on the African coast. *Palaver* now means something more than *palabra,* or "word." It can mean business or discussion or trouble. When "war palaver catch the country," people must fight, and some must die; and "woman palaver" often lands

a man in jail. *Pican* for baby or son or child comes from *pequeño* ("small") and *niño* ("child"). The two words flowed together in English speech to become first *picaninny* and then *pican*.

Read again an old story. Behold a new vision with sharper images. Sway with the rhythm of the storyteller. Feel the beat of the drums:

Long time past
Before you papa live
Before him papa live
Before him pa's papa live—

Long time past
Before them big tree live
Before them big tree's papa live—
That time God live.

EVERY MAN
HEART
LAY DOWN

Long time past
Before you papa live

Before him papa live
Before him pa's papa live—

Long time past
> Before them big tree live
> Before them big tree's papa live—

That time God live.

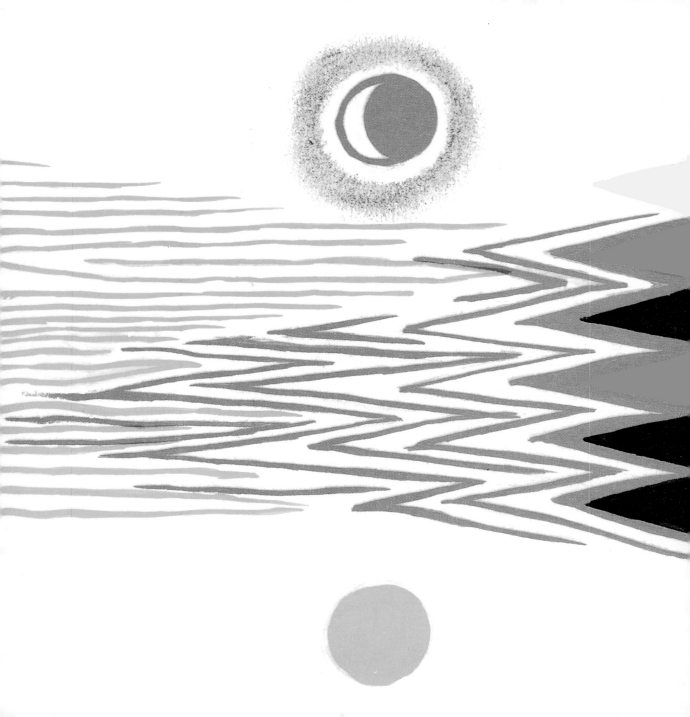

And God look on the world
What He done make
And Him heart no lay down.

And He walk about in the town
To see the people
And He sit down in the palaver house
To know the people
And He vex too much.

And God say
    "Nev mind.
    The people no hear My Word
    The people no walk My way
    Nev mind.

I going break the world and lose the people
I going make the day dark
And the night I going make hot.

I going make water that side where land belong
And land that side where water belong.
And I going make a new country
And make a new people."

Now this time
God's one small boy—Him small pican—hear God's word
And the pican grieve for people

So he go fore God's face
And make talk for him Pa.
     "Pa, I come for beg You," so he say
     "I come for beg You,
     Don't break the world
     What You done make.
     Don't lose the people
     What You done care for.
     I beg you
     Make it I go
     I talk to people
     I walk with people
     Bye-m-bye they savvy the way."

And the pican go down softly softly
And hold God's foot.
So God look on Him small boy
And Him heart be soft again

And God say
    "Aye My son,
When you beg me so
I no can vex.
Left me now, but hear me good:
If you go you must be born like a man
And you must live like a man
And you must have hurt and have hunger.

And hear me good:
Men will hate you
And they will flog you
And bye-m-bye they will kill you
And I no going put My hand there."

And the pican say
"I agree!"

And bye-m-bye God call Mary
To be ma for the pican.
Now Mary be new wife for Joseph
And Joseph ain't touch Mary self

So first time Joseph vex.
But God say
    "Nev mind, Joseph,
    This be God palaver."
And Joseph heart lay down.

And God see one king who try for do good
For all him people
And God say

"Ahah, Now I send My son
For be new king."
And God send star to call the king.

And in a far country
God hear a wise man call Him name
And God say to the wise man
    "I send My son to be a new wise man,
    Go now with the star."
And the star call
And the wise man follow.

And by the waterside
Men lay down for take rest

And they hear fine music in the sky
Like all the stars make song,
And they fear.

And all the dark make bright like day
And the water shine like fire
And no man can savvy
And they hearts turn over.

But God's angel come
And God's angel say
    "Make glad, all people,
      God's pican be born in Bethlehem."
And the people say "Oh."

And the wise man and the king
And the country people come to Bethlehem
And the star come low and stop.

But when they go for mansion house
The star no be there.
And when they go for Big Man's house
The star no be there.
And bye-m-bye when they go for hotel
The star no be there gain—

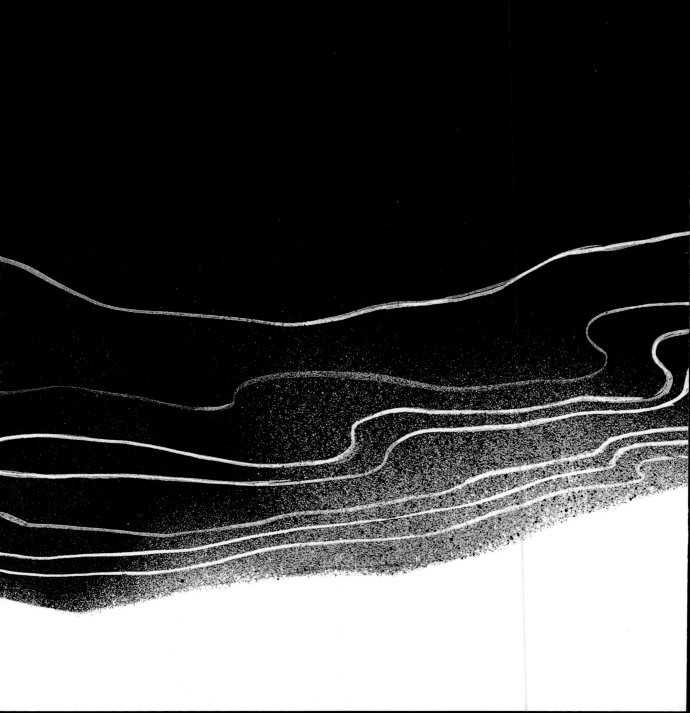

But the wise man say
       "Ahah, the star be by the small house
       Where cattle sleep!"
              And it was so.

And they find Joseph and Mary
And the small small pican
Fold up in country cloth

And the king bring gold for gift
And the wise man bring fine oil
And the country people bring new rice.

And they look on the God pican
And every man heart lay down.

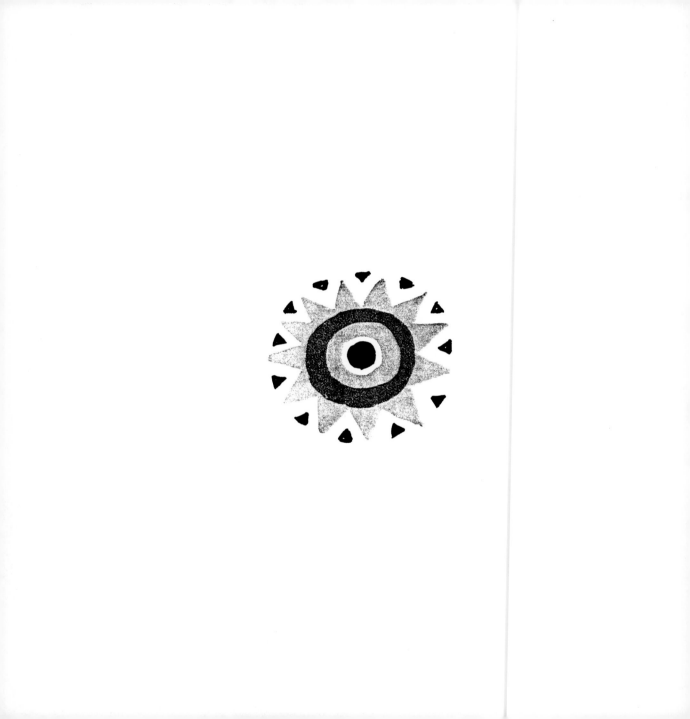